Thistle Broth

Written by Richard Thompson
Illustrated by Henry Fernandes

Orca Book Publishers

Old Thomas and Young Tom lived in a small cottage at the foot of a high and rocky hill.

One day in the fall, Old Thomas and his son were raking the leaves that had fallen from the maple tree in the yard, when a cold rain started to fall. They might have kept working except that a brisk wind started to blow as well. They bundled up their tools and ran into the cottage.

Old Thomas hung up his hat and, sitting himself down in his rocking chair, lit up his pipe. Young Tom took up a handful of kindling and started to lay a fire in the fireplace.

"Young Tom," said Old Thomas, "be a good lad and fetch some bread and cheese for my lunch."

"But Father," replied Young Tom, "I am busy lighting the fire. I can do only one thing at a time."

"Then do the most important thing first, Son!" declared Old Thomas. "It is more important to be warmed on the inside than to be toasted on the outside."

That seemed reasonable to Young Tom.

He put aside his fire lighting and went to the pantry to fetch cheese and bread. But as he was slicing the bread, water began to seep in through the roof. It dripped – plip-plop – onto the top of Old Thomas's bald head.

"Young Tom," said Old Thomas, "fetch a ladder and fix this leaking roof."

"But Father," said Young Tom, "I am busy making your lunch. I can do only one thing at a time."

"Then you must do the most important thing first, Son!" grumbled Old Thomas, as water dribbled over his forehead and collected in his eyebrows. "How can an old man enjoy his meal with cold water dripping onto his head?"

That seemed reasonable to Young Tom.

He put down the knife and went to fetch the ladder. As soon as he was gone, Old Thomas, sitting in the quiet of the empty cottage, noticed how mournfully the wind was moaning.

"Mercy!" he thought. "The wind is very, very ill."

He called to his son, and when Young Tom poked his head in at the door, the old man said, "Young Tom, go into the garden and gather some thistles. Make a weak broth to feed to the wind. It is very, very ill."

"But Father," said Young Tom, "I am busy fixing the roof. I can do only one thing at a time."

"Then you must do the most important thing first," muttered Old Thomas, as water dripped from the end of his nose. "Think, Young Tom! What is the discomfort of one old man compared to the suffering of the wind?"

That seemed reasonable to Young Tom.

He put down his tools and hurried to the garden. He picked an armful of thistles and brought them into the house. He put the thistles in a big black kettle with some water and put the kettle on the big black stove.

Soon the prickly aroma of boiled thistles filled the little cottage.

As Young Tom was stirring the thistle broth, the clouds burst open and the rain came down in torrents. Old Thomas saw the rain outside the window.

"Mercy!" he thought. "A monster has attacked the clouds and ripped them all to shreds."

"Young Tom," he said, "take the flannel bandages out of the medicine chest and go and bind up the clouds."

"But Father," said Young Tom, "I am busy making thistle broth for the wind. I can do only one thing at a time."

"Then do the most important thing first," grumped Old Thomas, shaking water out of his pipe. "What is the petty griping of the wind compared to the torment of the clouds?"

That seemed reasonable to Young Tom.

He left the broth burbling gently on the stove, then went and rummaged in the medicine chest for the bandages with which to bind the clouds.

With the bandages tucked inside his shirt, Young Tom went back into the storm. He saw immediately that he could not reach the clouds to bind them. He ran to the top of the high and rocky hill. Still the clouds tumbled far above his head.

He hurried back to the cottage and fetched his tools. In another trip, he fetched lumber and nails. And he began to build a ladder to reach the clouds.

He worked all day.

By evening his ladder was long enough. Young Tom began to climb. When he reached the top of the ladder, his head poked through the clouds and into the clear night above. Young Tom was reaching inside his shirt for the bandages with which to bind the clouds when he noticed the moon. Half of it was missing!

Young Tom hurried down the ladder and back to the cottage to tell his father what he had seen.

"Mercy!" said Old Thomas. "The moon will surely die with so large a hole in his side. Take an awl from the shed and a roll of twine. Sew up the moon before any more can fall away."

"But Father, I am busy bandaging the clouds," said Young Tom. "I can do only one thing at a time."

"Then you must do the most important thing first," mumbled Old Thomas, emptying water out of his boots. "What are a few ripped clouds compared to a dying moon?"

That seemed reasonable to Young Tom.

He fetched an awl and a ball of twine from the shed. He ran back to the top of the hill, took up his hammer, climbed to the top of the ladder and started building again.

When the ladder was almost to the moon, Young Tom was aghast to see stars falling from the sky, trailing light behind them across the blackness of the night.

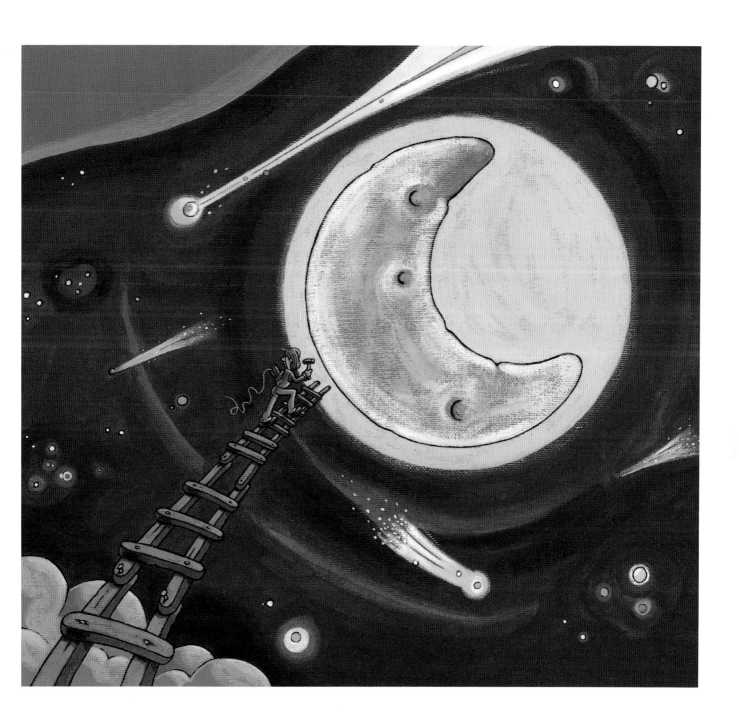

He hurried down the ladder and ran back to the cottage to tell his father what he had seen.

"Mercy!" declared Old Thomas. "If the sky falls apart we will surely all die. Young Tom, take some tar from the barrel in the tool shed and stick the stars back onto the sky."

"But Father," said Young Tom, "I am busy sewing up the moon. I can do only one thing at a time."

"Then you must do the most important thing first," quavered Old Thomas, wringing out his socks and shivering like a drowned dog. "What good is the moon at all, fixed or broken, if the sky falls apart around it?"

That seemed reasonable to Young Tom.

He opened the door and prepared to go out into the storm once more. But then he looked back at his poor soaked and shivering father.

"If I can do only one thing at a time," he said to himself, "I must do the most important thing first. And, surely, my father is more important to me than a few old stars."

He closed the door.

"What are you doing, Young Tom?" protested Old Thomas, between chattering teeth.

Young Tom put a match to the fire that he had laid earlier. He picked his old father up, chair and all, and moved him closer to the blaze. He fixed a plate with bread and cheese. He ladled out a bowlful of the thistle broth and brewed some tea to go with it. Soon the fire and the food and the hot drink had revived Old Thomas.

"I must admit that I do feel a sight better for some grub and a warm fire, Young Tom," said Old Thomas. He took out his pipe and rocked back in his chair. "But you'd better look to that broken sky, don't you think?"

Young Tom remembered the sky that was falling apart and the broken moon. He remembered the wounded clouds and the ailing wind.

He rushed out into the yard.

But the wind was still. The clouds had all but disappeared. The moon had set in the west. And a fat golden sun was chasing the stars from the sky in the east.

Young Tom breathed a sigh of relief and went to finish fixing the roof.

Text copyright © 1992 Richard Thompson
Illustrations copyright © 1992 Henry Fernandes

Publication assistance provided by The Canada Council.
All rights reserved.

Orca Book Publishers
PO Box 5626 Stn. B
Victoria, B.C. Canada
V8R 6S4

Design by Christine Toller
Printed and bound in Hong Kong

Canadian Cataloguing in Publication Data
Thompson, Richard, 1951–
Thistle broth

ISBN 0-920501-85-0

I. Fernandes, Henry. II. Title.
PS8589.H64T5 1992   jC813'.54   C92-091500-0
PZ7.T496Th 1992